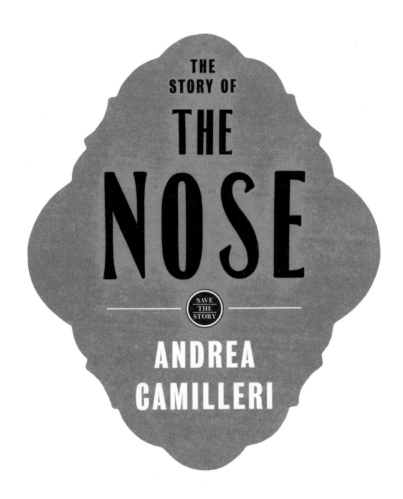

THE STORY OF

THE
NOSE

SAVE THE STORY

ANDREA CAMILLERI

ILLUSTRATED BY MAJA CELIJA

Translated by Stephen Sartarelli

PUSHKIN CHILDREN'S BOOKS

Pushkin Children's Books
71-75 Shelton Street
London, WC2H 9JQ

The Story of The Nose first published in Italian as
La storia de Il Naso
© 2010 Gruppo Editoriale L'Espresso S.p.A
and © 2010 Andrea Camilleri. All rights reserved.

This edition published by Pushkin Children's Books in 2014

ISBN 978 1 782690 17 7

Set in Garamond Premier Pro by Tetragon, London

Printed and bound in Italy by Printer Trento SRL
on Munken Print Cream 115gsm

www.pushkinpress.com

THE
STORY OF

THE

NOSE

One

I must begin with a disclaimer. Dear readers, the idea of retelling, in my own words, a story such as Nikolai Gogol's "The Nose" probably seems an act of mindless immodesty, like a lame person attempting to race against the world champion in the 100-metre dash.

In my first year of elementary school, in 1931 (!!!), the teacher, in handwriting class, had me making strokes—that is, vertical marks that had to be perfectly straight. Well, I feel as though I'm still trying to get my strokes straight, whereas Gogol bequeathed three or four masterpieces to the world. In choosing this particular story to retell, I must confess I also did so out of laziness. In my mind I was thinking that it's one thing to retell a short story, and something else entirely to preserve, in just a few pages, the story of, say, *The Iliad*, or Manzoni's *The Betrothed*. But I'd miscalculated, because the short story is rather like the game of pick-up-sticks:

it takes only one wrong move to mess the whole thing up.

So how did I do it? Well, I moved about inside Gogol's tale with the same cautious trepidation that the author's petty clerks moved about in those ministry halls, on tiptoe, holding their breath so as not to disturb the boss...

All right, no more stalling. Time to buck up. This is the story of a nose that, after disappearing inexplicably from the face of its legitimate owner, took on a life of its own. How odd! you say. Not at all! Literature, mind you, is full of this sort of thing. One author imagined a killer's severed hand that carried on killing, while another amused himself telling of the severed head of a victim of the guillotine that continued to talk... Normally they're horror stories that send chills down your spine. Gogol's story has instead the merit of being quite funny. Which is saying a lot.

It all began at dawn on 25th March 1832, in St Petersburg, which at the time was the capital of Russia, when Ivan Yakovlevich, a barber by trade, woke up unusually early, and the first thing he noticed was the tantalizing aroma of warm, fresh-baked bread.

This was nothing new. At that hour every street in the city was filled with the scent of crispy buns. He sat up slightly in bed and saw that his stern, respectable consort, Praskovya Osipovna, was at that moment taking a good number of buns out of the oven. Ivan made a quick decision.

"I don't feel like coffee this morning," he said to his wife. "I'd rather have buns with onions."

Truth be told, he would have liked first to have a good cup of coffee and then enjoy the buns and onions, but he knew that he could never have asked Praskovya for both things at once, because his wife had no tolerance for such excessive demands.

Excellent, Praskovya thought to herself, being rather fond of coffee. *The fool can have all the buns and onions he wants; that way I can drink his share of coffee.* And she put a bun on the table.

You could say a lot about Ivan, but not that he was immodest. Indeed, he got up and, before sitting

down to breakfast, put on his coat which, at the time, was the common work coat worn by barbers. He then sat down at the table, put the salt cellar near his plate, cleaned two onions, grabbed a knife and, with an expression of inspired bliss, cut the bun in half.

And immediately, to his amazement, he noticed that there was a foreign body in the middle of the bun, a white sort of thing. Bringing the tip of the knife to it, he nudged it. Then he touched it with his index finger. It was a solid mass. But, try as he might, he couldn't imagine what it was. Reaching out with his forefinger and thumb, he seized the thing, pulled it out of the bun, and looked at it.

It was a nose.

There was no doubt about it. A fleshy, man's nose. A well-shaped nose.

In his astonishment, he immediately dropped the nose. He couldn't believe his eyes, which he quickly shut and began to rub. When he reopened them, the nose was still there. He touched it. It was a nose, there was no denying it. An actual nose! And the more he looked at it, the more he realized that it was in fact, so to speak, a familiar nose, one that he'd had some sort of dealings with.

His face became etched with terror. His wife came running and saw the whitish thing on the table.

"What's *that*?" she asked.

"A nose."

Praskovya became indignant and turned red in the face.

"You rascal! You drunkard! Whose nose did you cut off! Eh? I'm going to report you to the police!"

The barber was about to protest, but his wife hissed at him.

"Silence, scoundrel! People have told me that when you shave your clients' beards you manhandle their noses and they don't know how they manage to remain attached!"

Ivan felt his heart sink, because he'd just recognized the nose. It belonged to an important man, Major Kovalev, whom he shaved every Wednesday and Sunday.

"Stop, Praskovya!" Ivan pleaded. "Do you want to ruin me? Look, I'll wrap it up in a rag and stick it in a corner, and then take it with me when I go out."

"Out of the question!" his wife screeched. "I refuse to be in the same room as a cut-off nose! Now get out!"

Ivan was unable to move, beset as he was by all the questions crowding his brain. How could this have happened? Had he come home drunk the previous evening or hadn't he? And how could one explain the fact that the bun was cooked, but not the nose? Praskovya, meanwhile, kept on yelling, undaunted.

"Good-for-nothing rascal! If you don't get moving, I'm going to call the police!"

Ivan began to tremble, imagining the police with their big boots, silver-brocaded collars and swords, interrogating him with their terrifying scowls and accusing him of having stolen a nose...

At last he summoned the strength to stand up. He put on his boots, wrapped the nose in a rag and went out. He planned to get rid of the nose as soon as the opportunity arose, throwing it away behind a kerbstone or into a doorway, or even by simply dropping it onto the ground and then turning down the first alley he came across. But that morning, as if by design, he only ran into people he knew, who asked him where he was headed or whom he was going off to shave in such a hurry. In short, he never found the right moment.

Then, at last, as soon as the street seemed half deserted, he managed to rid himself of the little bundle, nonchalantly letting it drop to the ground. But a police officer suddenly appeared and scolded him severely, ordering him to pick up what he'd dropped. Ivan obeyed without breathing a word. Meanwhile he grew more and more glum and desperate, as the stores and shops began to open and the streets grew busier. Then the solution to his troubling problem occurred to him. It was quite simple. He merely had to go to the nearest bridge and throw the nose into the river.

He headed off at a fast pace.

Two

As he is walking towards the bridge, I will take the opportunity to tell you that Ivan Yakovlevich, like every self-respecting Russian tradesman, was an incorrigible drunkard. And he was not a handsome man. Although he shaved other men's noses daily, the hairs on his own red nose remained eternally unshaven. The overcoat he wore was patchy, in the sense that, while it was indeed black, it was covered with yellowish and greenish spots, the collar was threadbare, and in the place of the three buttons had only three strands of dangling thread.

Every time he sat down in the chair for a shave, Major Kovalev would say:

"Ivan, your hands always stink!"

"Why would they stink?" the barber would ask.

"I don't know; I just know that they stink."

And Ivan, after snorting a pinch of snuff, would start lathering the Major all over, out of spite, even in spots where there was no need, and took great pleasure in so doing.

Reaching the bridge, Ivan looked around several times, leant out over the parapet as if to count the fish passing under the arches and, feeling reassured, cast the bundle with the nose into the water. He immediately felt great relief. He even broke into a big grin. Indeed he felt so happy that, instead of going to the shop to shave his customers, he decided to give himself a treat. Spotting the sign of an inn that served food and tea, he craved some piping-hot punch, and headed in that direction. But then, to his horror, he noticed a municipal policeman with a three-cornered hat and bushy sideburns pointing at him and gesturing for him to approach.

He immediately doffed his cap and ran towards the officer.

"Good morning and good health, your excellency!" he said humbly, bowing.

"Forget the excellency crap and explain to me what you were doing on the bridge!"

"I'm a barber, and I was just on my way to open up my shop. I stopped on the bridge to watch the water coursing by below."

"Stop talking rubbish! What were you doing?"

Blanching in fear, Ivan tried to ingratiate himself with the policeman. He declared that he was willing to shave him three times a week, free of charge. The officer glared at him disdainfully.

"For your information, I've already got three barbers, that's three, who shave me free of charge, and they consider it an honour! Now, out with it! Tell me what you were doing."

Ivan grew even paler.

But here I must stop. Because I cannot reveal any of what was said between the barber and the officer. If I did so now, it would be, so to speak, a narrative mistake. I'll talk about it later, in due time. At any rate Ivan Yakovlevich is not an important character. A second-rate figure, his only merit is to have found a nose inside a bun. Might it not be better, at this point, if I described instead the personality of the nose's owner, that is Major Kovalev?

First of all, you should know that Major Kovalev was not actually a major, but a public official with the title of "collegiate assessor". Since his rank was equivalent to that of a major in the army, he had people call him "Major" to give himself more lustre and prestige. And we certainly won't do him wrong by calling him anything else.

The Major was usually impeccably dressed. The collar of his shirt was always immaculate and starched. His bushy sideburns covered a good half of his cheeks and came right up under his nose. He customarily wore a great many medals with noble coats of arms inscribed on them, or words such as "Wednesday", "Thursday", "Monday" and so on. The Major was a bachelor, but would not have been averse to marriage, so long as his bride came with a dowry of no less than 200,000 roubles.

He liked to parade himself down Nevsky Prospekt every day of the week.

And here I cannot help but say a few words about this wonderful street. Nevsky Prospekt, in St Petersburg. All of it. I am certain that not a single one of its pale, white-collar inhabitants would trade Nevsky Prospekt for all the treasures on earth. The twenty-five-year-olds with magnificent moustaches and perfectly tailored frock coats, and the old men with white hairs sprouting from their chins, and heads as bald as a silver platter: all go into raptures at the sight of Nevsky Prospekt.

And what about the ladies? Ah, for the ladies, Nevsky Prospekt is an even greater source of pleasure. And for whom, indeed, is it not pleasurable? The instant you set foot on Nevsky Prospekt, you breathe only an air of promenade...

And how many Gogol characters have travelled down Nevsky Prospekt! Here we see the miserable little clerk, Akaky Akakievich, who, having managed to buy himself a new overcoat through tremendous sacrifice, has it stolen from him, dies of sorrow, and becomes a ghost, haunting the street and compelling passers-by to take off their coats...

And look, farther ahead we see the modest landowner Chichikov, running from one ministry to another. He's learnt that the government is giving out large subsidies for the repopulation of rural areas, and is trying to buy up those famous "dead souls"— that is, all those peasants who died after the great census but have not yet been registered as dead by the records office and who, as living persons, will serve the great swindle Chichikov has in mind.

A bit farther on, right near the bridge where Ivan the barber was stopped by the policeman, you can see the foppish Khlestakov, still a bit dazed from all the unexpected honours and homages heaped on him in a nearby provincial city. Mistaken for a government inspector—a sort of financial authority—for a few days he became the centre of attention for the rich and powerful of the province, who tried to corrupt him and win him over to their side.

But enough of this. If I keep talking about Nevsky Prospekt, we'll never get back to our subject.

Three

That morning the Major woke up early and, flapping his lips, said *Brrr!* He always did this upon awakening, but didn't know why. He stretched, yawned, called the manservant and ordered him to hold up the little mirror that was on the table. He wanted to check a little pimple that had sprouted on his nose the day before.

This was how he came to notice, to his great astonishment, that there was a void—or, more accurately, a perfectly smooth space—in the place of his nose. In terror, the Major leapt out of bed, went and washed his eyes, then looked in the mirror again. No nose. He began pinching himself to see if he was still asleep. No, he

was not asleep. No nose. He shook himself violently. It was no use.

No nose.

He got dressed in a hurry, having decided to go straight to the chief of police. An utterly logical decision. Indeed, that was where one reported thefts and disappearances.

To his dismay, there were no cabs on the street, and he was forced to go on foot, wrapping himself up in his cape and covering his face with a handkerchief, as if he had a nosebleed. Meanwhile he was thinking that his nose could not have disappeared so inexplicably, and that it must be his imagination. Thus, passing in front of a pastry shop, he went inside to look at himself in the mirror. There were only waiters about, still half asleep, sweeping the floor. He went up to a large mirror and looked at himself. No, it was not his imagination. He no longer had a nose. The Major spat on the floor in disgust at the sight of that empty space in the middle of his face.

"If only there was at least some little thing in its place!" he exclaimed in anger. "But there's nothing!"

He left the shop and, contrary to habit—normally he was always affable with everyone—did not look or

smile at anybody. At one point, he paused in front of a doorway. An inexplicable phenomenon was unfolding before his terrified eyes. A carriage had stopped right in front of him and, after the coachman had opened the door, a man in uniform darted out, quickly slipped into the doorway, and disappeared from view. But Kovalev had enough time to recognize him and, in his horror and shock, had frozen like a statue.

That man was his nose!

Seeing such an unusual spectacle, Kovalev's sight began to dim, and he could barely stand on his feet; still, he decided to wait, whatever the cost, for the nose to return to the carriage. What he had witnessed had upset him, and he was sweating and trembling all over.

Two minutes later, the nose came back out. It was wearing a gold-embroidered uniform with a high, stiff collar, high suede boots and a sword at its side. To judge from the variegated plumes in its hat, it appeared to be a state councillor.

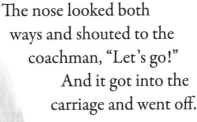

The nose looked both ways and shouted to the coachman, "Let's go!"

And it got into the carriage and went off.

Poor Kovalev very nearly went mad.

How could it be that this nose, which until yesterday had been on his face, and which theoretically should have been unable either to walk or to ride in a carriage, was now wearing the uniform of a state councillor?

He started running after the carriage, which luckily did not go far and stopped in front of Kazan Cathedral.

Four

I'm sorry, but here I must make a slight digression. When, in 1835, Gogol wanted to publish this story, he had to submit it to the Tsar's censors, as required. They decided that the carriage should not stop in front of the cathedral, which was too august a place to be the setting for Kovalev's encounter with his nose, however disguised as a state councillor. They said it would be an insult to the religion.

And so Gogol suggested that the meeting take place in a Catholic church; that way there would be no slight to the Russian Orthodox religion. It is still a holy place, the censors retorted; it's better if the meeting occurs in a public place. Poor Gogol had no choice but to give in, and moved the meeting to the Gostiny Dvor, the great indoor market on Nevsky Prospekt.

At this point the censors added that it would be more respectful of the authorities if Major Kovalev did not take his problem to the chief of police, who was too important a personage, but went instead to see a simple functionary. And Gogol again complied. At last he could send his story to a literary review. Which sent it back to him claiming that the story was "vulgar and trivial".

Now, if you find Gogol's story of the nose absurd, don't you find the censors' observations even more absurd, though far less amusing? But let us proceed.

Kovalev rushed towards the portal of the cathedral, making his way through a crowd of beggars. Inside, there were only a handful of people praying, most of them standing near the entrance. The Major was in such a frantic state that he didn't even have the strength to pray; he looked everywhere for the man he was trying to find. At last he spotted him, standing apart from the congregants. The nose was hiding the rest of its face inside the high, stiff collar, and praying with a rather devout expression.

"How can I approach him?" Kovalev wondered anxiously. "Everything about him, the hat, the uniform, shows that he's a state councillor. Won't he be offended if I disturb him?"

He drew near to him and began clearing his throat, but the nose did not for a second abandon its pious attitude, and in fact started genuflecting deeply.

Summoning all his strength, Kovalev bucked up and addressed the nose.

"Esteemed sir, I—"

"What do you want?" the nose brusquely interrupted him, turning towards him. "Can't you see I'm praying?"

The Major lost his train of thought.

"Well, I, ahem, wanted to say that, well, it seems strange to me, your excellency... I mean, you should know your proper place! Whereas you disappear just like that, and where do I find you? In a church! You must admit..."

The nose looked at him, taken aback.

"I have no idea what you're talking about. Please speak more clearly."

Speak more clearly? Easier said than done!

Plucking up his courage again, Kovalev told him that he was a major, and that it was therefore

unseemly for a man of his position to go around
without a nose. He added that being seen without
a nose might be acceptable to someone of the lower
classes, to a merchant or peasant, but for someone
who was not only a major, but about to be made
a governor... He informed him, moreover, that he
frequented the homes of many high-ranking figures
and was a friend of Madame Chektareva, the wife of a
state councillor...

"And so, esteemed sir," he concluded, "you may
judge for yourself. I do not know whether you
consider such conduct in keeping with principles
of duty and honour, but if I do you the courtesy of
speaking more clearly, you must understand..."

Before continuing, the Major summoned all his
dignity.

"Esteemed sir," Kovalev said. "I do not know how
to take your words... The matter seems perfectly clear.
You... You are my nose!"

The nose looked at the Major and raised its
eyebrows.

"You are very seriously mistaken, good sir! What
has got into you? I am here on my own. And there
can, moreover, be no connection between us. To

judge from the buttons on your uniform, you serve in a different bureau."

So saying, he turned and resumed praying devoutly.

Not knowing what to do or think, Kovalev fell into a state of profound confusion.

Five

At that moment he heard the pleasant rustle of a woman's dress. Kovalev turned around. Not far from him was an elderly lady adorned in lace, and beside her a slender young woman in a white dress elegantly wrapped around her slim waist, wearing a small straw hat as light as a cream puff.

Behind the ladies was a hussar, a cavalry officer, who came to a sudden halt and opened his snuffbox. He was tall, with enormous sideburns and a good dozen high collars. The Major approached, fixed the batiste collar of his shirt, adjusted the medals hanging from their gold chain and, smiling to the left and right, at last set his eyes on the slender lady, who

was leaning to one side like a young spring blossom, the delicate fingers of her little white hand touching her forehead.

The smile on Kovalev's face further broadened when he noticed, under the young woman's little hat, a strikingly white, roundish chin, and part of a cheek suffused with the colour of the first rose of spring. But then he abruptly took a step back as though he had burnt himself, remembering that there was absolutely nothing in the place where his nose should have been. His eyes filled with tears. He turned around, ready to tell the man who passed himself off as a state councillor that he was a fraud and a scoundrel and nothing but a nose, his nose…

But the nose was no longer there. It had managed to slip away. Falling into the darkest despair, Kovalev ran out and stopped for a moment under the colonnade, looking carefully in every direction for the nose. He had a clear memory of the plumed hat and the gold-embroidered uniform, but hadn't noticed what kind of overcoat the nose was wearing. Nor the colour of his carriage or the horses, or whether he had some sort of servant in livery following behind it. Carriages, after all, went by so fast that not only was it hard to tell them apart, but even had he been able to recognize the nose's carriage, he would have had no chance of stopping it.

It was a beautiful, sunny day. There were countless people on Nevsky Prospekt, a veritable floral cascade of ladies scattered all across the sidewalks. Lo and behold, he saw a court councillor of his acquaintance, whom he called "Colonel", especially in front of strangers. And there was also Yarizhkin, Chief Clerk at the Senate, a good friend, who was a terrible gambler. And here was another major who had just been made assessor and was gesturing to him to approach... But Kovalev could hardly let them see him without a nose. Feeling profoundly unhappy, Kovalev stopped a free carriage and asked to be taken to the chief of police. He climbed aboard and for the entire journey did nothing but spur the coachman on, shouting:

"Hurry! Hurry!"

Upon entering the lobby, he shouted to the porter:
"Is the chief of police in?"

"No sir, he just went out."

"This is all I need!" the Major exclaimed.

"If you'd come just a minute earlier, you might
have found him in," the porter said philosophically.

Without once removing the handkerchief from
his face, Kovalev got back into the coach and started
shouting desperately.

"Go! Go!"

"Where to?" the coachman asked.

"Straight ahead!"

"What do you mean, 'straight ahead'? The road
forks here: should I go right or left?"

"Stop!" ordered the Major. And he began to
reflect.

He realized it would be pointless to seek justice
from administrative officials of the same ilk as his
nose claimed to be. It was already clear to him from
their conversation that the nose held nothing in the
world sacred. And it was therefore quite likely that
it had had the gall to lie to him straight-faced in
this case.

Given the situation, it might be best to address
the Vice Bureau, since they were more in the habit of
taking swift action than other bureaus. He was about
to tell the cabby to take him there when it occurred
to him that the fraud and scoundrel might now be
easily fleeing the city, with the advantage he had
gained. And all his searching would either be in vain
or drag on for a long time.

Six

At last Kovalev had what seemed to him a brilliant idea. He decided to go to the editorial offices of a newspaper and publish an ad so that anyone who might see his nose could inform him and tell him where it was.

He ordered the coachman to head towards the newspaper's office, all the while pounding the coachman's back with his fists, shouting: "Faster, you rascal! Faster, scoundrel!"

At last the coach stopped, and Kovalev, out of breath, entered the newspaper's small, dark waiting room. There was an elderly, bespectacled clerk sitting behind a desk, counting copper coins with a pen between his teeth.

"Where does one submit advertisements?" Kovalev asked, yelling the question.

"And a good day to you too, sir," said the clerk, momentarily looking up before returning to his stacks of coins.

"I would like to publish..." the Major began.

The clerk, without looking at him, asked him to wait a moment and then began writing down some figures in a register with his right hand, while moving a few little balls on an abacus with two fingers of his left.

All around the desk were a great many old women, salesmen, merchants and porters with notes in their hands on which were written the most motley assortments of advertisements for publication, whose offerings for sale went from a little-used carriage imported from Paris in 1814 to turnip and radish seeds, a small country house, a sixteen-year-old do-it-all maid, a seventeen-year-old horse and a gig without a single spring.

With all these people crowded together in the room, the air was quite unpleasant, but Kovalev could not smell the strong odour because his nose was long gone. After a spell, the Major became impatient. With great pique he told the clerk that his case was different and urgent, and that he had no more time to waste.

"Straight away! Straight away!" the clerk replied. And he started throwing receipts in the faces of the old ladies and porters, yelling: "You, two roubles, forty kopeks! You, one rouble sixty!"

When they were all gone, he asked the Major what he wanted.

"A bit of roguery or fraud has occurred, I still haven't quite figured it out," said Kovalev. "I would like to publish an advertisement stating that anyone who can give me any information about the scoundrel will be duly rewarded."

"All right," said the clerk. "Would you please tell me your name?"

"Why do you want to know?" the Major replied. "I'm terribly sorry, but I can't tell you. I have many important acquaintances, you know, Madame Chektareva, the wife of the state councillor, and Pelagea Grigorievna Podtochina, the wife of the staff officer... If they were ever to find out, God help me! No, no... Write simply, 'a man with the rank of major'..."

"Was the one who escaped a servant of yours?" the clerk asked.

"What, a servant?" Kovalev wondered, perplexed. Could his nose be considered a servant? But the disappearance of any servant would be far less serious than that of a nose. He decided to explain matters.

"No, it's my nose that ran off."

"What a strange surname!" the clerk muttered to himself. Then he asked: "Did this Nozoff steal a large sum of money from you?"

At this point Kovalev started shouting in exasperation.

"You haven't understood a thing! I'm talking about my nose, not any Nozoff! Are you listening? My nose! Which has disappeared and only the devil knows where it's gone!"

"Your nose? But, 'disappeared' in what way? There's something I don't understand," the clerk said suspiciously.

The Major clenched his teeth and forced himself to remain calm.

"I don't know how it disappeared. What matters is that now it's going around town dressed up as a state councillor. And I therefore would like you to publish that whosoever captures it should bring it to me at once. Judge for yourself: how can I go on without a nose? It's not like your little toe, which remains inside your shoe and so nobody can see whether it's there or not. You see, every Thursday I pay a call on the councillor's wife Madame Chektareva; and Madame Podtochina, the staff officer's wife, who also has a pretty daughter, is likewise a close acquaintance of mine... And now I cannot show my face to them."

The clerk, in no way moved by Kovalev's words, reflected for a moment, then shook his head and said that, no, he could not publish such an advertisement in his newspaper. The Major had been expecting just such an answer.

"And why not?" he asked, beside himself.

"It would put the newspaper's reputation at risk," the clerk explained. "If someone wrote that his nose

had run away, you understand… We already have complaints that we print too many absurdities and false rumours."

The Major got upset. He was a man who was full of himself, and therefore extremely sensitive. How dared this petty clerk deem his story absurd?

"And what, in your opinion, is so absurd about what has happened to me?" he asked provocatively.

"You just *think* it's not there!" the clerk retorted. And he went on to tell him that the previous week, a man had published an advertisement stating that a black poodle had run away. And then it turned out that the black poodle was actually the cashier of an important credit institute.

"It's not a black poodle I wish to advertise, but my own nose! As if I were advertising myself!" Kovalev pointed out.

The clerk shook his head.

"But my nose really *has* disappeared!" the Major insisted. "Look for yourself," he added, removing the handkerchief from his face.

"That is strange indeed, very strange," said the clerk. "The area is perfectly smooth. Like a pancake just out of the pan."

"So can you see that I absolutely must publish my advertisement?"

"That could, perhaps, be arranged," said the clerk. "But I'm convinced it will do no good. Perhaps you should address some journal that deals in natural phenomena or the education of the young."

The Major fell silent, discouraged. The clerk tried to reassure him.

"I am truly sorry such a thing has happened to you, believe me. Would you like a pinch of snuff? It gets rid of headaches and is good for haemorrhoids."

So saying, he held out the snuffbox and dexterously lifted the lid. The Major lost his temper.

"I fail to understand how you can joke about such a matter! Can't you see that I'm missing precisely what is needed to take your snuff? The devil take you!"

And he left, deeply irritated, and headed towards the home of the district's Police Commissar. Who, at that moment, having had his cook remove his boots after a day of hard, thankless work, was getting to savour the pleasures of domestic peace and quiet. Kovalev's visit was thus rather untimely. The Commissar listened coldly to the Major's story, and then pointed out to him that right after lunch was not the time to open an investigation, as nature had herself established that, after sating oneself, a nice little nap was in order. And he added that, in his opinion, a truly respectable man does not lose his nose just like that, and that, at any rate, there were a great many majors around with dirty laundry who frequented places of ill repute.

Kovalev felt deeply resentful. Not only could he not tolerate what the Commissar was saying about him as a man, but he really couldn't stand to hear his title or rank invoked. He even believed that at the theatre one could allow slights of non-commissioned officers, but one must never attack officers. And so he shook his head and said in a most dignified manner:

"I have nothing to add to your offensive remarks!"

And he left and went home. His apartment seemed sad and squalid to him. On the dirty sofa in the ante-room lay his manservant Ivan, spitting at the ceiling and always hitting, with great skill, the same spot. Kovalev flew into a rage and struck him on the forehead. The servant hastened to help the Major off with his cape. Going into his bedroom, Kovalev, tired and unhappy, dropped into an armchair and began sighing.

"If only I had lost an arm or a leg," he thought to himself, "it would have been better. Even being without ears would be more tolerable. But a man without a nose is not a man! If at least it had been cut off in battle or in a duel... but to disappear for no reason... No, it makes no sense for a nose to disappear! Surely I'm dreaming, or hallucinating. Perhaps I drank vodka instead of water and am now completely drunk. Yes, that must be it. But I'd better check."

And to confirm, he pinched himself painfully. It hurt so much, he became convinced he was perfectly sober and lucid. He got up from the armchair and looked at himself in

the mirror, in the hope of seeing his nose back in its
place.

But no.

How was this possible? A button's disappearance,
or a silver spoon's, was understandable. But a nose!
And right there in his own apartment! He collapsed
into the armchair, devastated.

Seven

A suspicion suddenly came over him: it was all the fault of that high official's wife, Madame Podtochina. She wanted him to marry her daughter, even though he wished to avoid a definitive engagement. When the official's wife had openly admitted to him that she wanted to marry her daughter off to him, he had backtracked, saying he was still too young and would rather make a career for himself first.

So the official's wife, in revenge, had decided to ruin him and surely enlisted some sorceress who had made his nose disappear. Yes, that must be what had happened. But what to do now? Should he file a complaint against her, or pay a call on her and unmask her?

Meanwhile Ivan entered with a candle in hand. Kovalev grabbed his handkerchief and covered his face. As soon as the servant went out, he heard a voice from the ante-room.

"Does Major Kovalev live here?"

"Come in. I'm over here," the Major said, standing up.

A municipal police officer in a tricorn hat came in. A good-looking man. Would you like to know who he was? Well, I don't want to keep you in suspense. He was the same policeman who had stopped the barber Ivan Yakovlevich on the bridge as he was on his way to drink some hot punch. Remember?

"I'm sorry, but did you lose a nose?" the officer asked politely.

"I certainly did," the Major affirmed sadly.

"It is my pleasure to tell you that it's been found," the policeman said.

"What?!" the Major shouted incredulously.

"Your nose was stopped while trying to flee. It had boarded a

stagecoach headed to Riga and showed a passport bearing the name of a clerk. The strangest thing about it all was that even I, when I had it in front of me, took it for a gentleman! Luckily I had my eyeglasses with me and immediately saw that it was only a nose. I'm quite near-sighted, you know, and if you stand before me, all I can see is that you have a face, but I can't make anything out in it: the beard, the nose, nothing... My mother-in-law—my wife's mother, that is—can't see at all."

Kovalev was beside himself with excitement.

"Where is it? Where is it? I must go there at once!"

"Please don't worry. Knowing how much you needed it, I brought it with me. The strangest thing is that the main culprit is a rascally barber whom we've now got in custody. I'd suspected him for some time of drunkenness and theft. Well, anyway, here's your nose, just as it was before," the officer concluded, extracting the nose from his pocket and setting it down on the table.

"That's it! That's really it!" the Major shouted for joy. Then, in a burst of hospitality: "Do let me make you some tea."

"Thank you, but I really can't. You know, the cost of foodstuffs has gone up tremendously. My mother-in-law—my wife's mother, that is—also lives with us, and there are the children too... The oldest is very bright, but we haven't the means to send him to school..."

Getting the drift, Kovalev grabbed a red ten-rouble note and stuck it into the policeman's hand, and the officer withdrew with a deep bow.

It took Kovalev a couple of minutes to recover his faculties of sight and hearing. His sudden joy had the effect of numbing his senses. With extreme care, he picked up the nose with both hands and studied it attentively.

"There's the pimple that sprouted on the left side!" he exclaimed triumphantly.

Kovalev's elation was dampened by a sudden concern: what if the nose wouldn't stick to his face? He blanched. With a feeling of indescribable horror, he went up to a mirror, to avoid the risk of putting it back on crooked. His hands were trembling. With

supreme caution he placed the nose back in its place. He kept it pressed down for a while, then let go. He had to catch it in mid-air. Horrors! It wouldn't stick!

Then he brought it to his mouth, warmed it with his breath, and put it back in the empty space. But the nose wouldn't stay.

"Get back in your place, idiot!" he ordered it.

The nose seemed as though made of wood and fell onto the table with a strange noise, like that of a cork. The Major's face was twisted up in a tense grimace.

"Why won't it hold?" he asked himself in despair. It was no use. The moment he let go of it, the nose would fall back onto the table. And so he called for Ivan and sent him out to ask for help from a doctor who lived in the building.

The doctor arrived almost at once. After asking him how long ago the misfortune had befallen him, he grabbed the Major by the chin and thumped him hard with his thumb in the very place where Kovalev's nose used to be, whereupon the Major's head jerked back with such force that it struck the wall.

The doctor said it was nothing and, after pulling him away from the wall a little, had him turn his head to the right, felt the spot, looked where the nose used to be and said:

"Hmm!" Then he had him turn his head to the left and said:

"Hmm!"

To conclude, he thumped him with his thumb again, so that the Major leant his head back like a horse having its teeth examined. Having completed the test, he shook his head.

"It's better for you to remain the way you are. It could be reattached, of course, but I assure you, it would be worse for you."

"But what am I supposed to do without a nose?" asked Kovalev. "And, anyway, how could it possibly be any worse than this? Where can I go without a nose? I have many important acquaintances, you know, like Madame Chektareva—the state councillor's wife—Madame Podtochina—wife of a high staff official—although after everything she's done to me

I don't think I'll want to have any more to do with her, except perhaps through the intermediary of the police. But please, do replace my nose, however you can, even poorly, so long as it sticks! I could perhaps hold it there in place during more difficult moments. At any rate I don't dance, which would probably be dangerous. And, as concerns the trouble you've gone to, rest assured that—"

"I never give care out of self-interest," the doctor interrupted him in a gentle but firm voice. "It's against my principles. And if I have people pay me after every visit, it is to avoid offending my patients by refusing. I could reattach your nose, but I assure you it will make things worse. Wash yourself often with cold water, and you'll be perfectly fine without a nose. As for the nose, I advise you to put it in alcohol in a jar—two tablespoons of vodka and warmed-up vinegar. You could get a tidy little sum for it, you know. If you want, I'll buy it myself."

"No! No! It's not for sale!" Kovalev cried desperately. "I would rather it were lost!"

"Well, I'm sorry," the doctor said coldly. "I was only trying to be helpful."

And he walked gravely out of the room.

Eight

The following morning, before submitting his complaint, Kovalev made a point of writing to Madame Podtochina, asking her to do, without any arguments, what she must to make his nose cease being so recalcitrant and return to its proper place. Here is the letter the Major sent to the wife of the general staff officer:

My good Aleksandra Grigorievna!
I fail to understand your manner of behaviour. In acting this way, you gain nothing and are unable to force me to marry your daughter. You must believe me when I tell you that I know everything about the matter with my nose, just as I know that you are the principal, indeed the only, person responsible. Its sudden, inexplicable departure from its proper place, its attempt to escape and disguise itself as a high official, are nothing more than the

consequences of the magic spells you have woven. For
my part, it behoves me to warn you that if the nose in
question is not reattached to its place this very day, I
shall have no choice but to turn to the authorities.

With utmost esteem, I remain your faithful servant.

Platon Kovalev

Madame Podtochina's reply came at once.

Good Platon Kuzmich,

I find your letter quite astonishing. I confess in all
sincerity that I should never have expected it of you.
The reproaches you level at me are unfair. I have never
received the high official you mention into my home,
neither disguised nor in his natural guise. And you
speak as well of a nose. If by this you mean that I am
thumbing my nose at you—or, in other words, refusing
you my daughter's hand—I am astounded at your
assertion. For I have never been opposed to it, and if
you now wish to become engaged to my daughter, I am
ready to consent at once. With this hope in mind, I
remain forever ready to serve you,

Aleksandra Podtochina

Reading Madame Podtochina's letter, Kovalev had to admit to himself that the staff official's wife seemed to be entirely unapprised of the situation. And so he began to wonder how and in what circumstances the problem could have occurred. He turned it over and over again in his mind, racking his brains. And, naturally, he arrived at no conclusion. Meanwhile, as always happens, rumours about the strange event quickly spread across the capital.

During this same period people had become interested in unusual events, inexplicable phenomena such as the case of the chairs that had suddenly started dancing in Konyushennaya Street. It therefore came as no surprise to anyone when the rumour began to spread that Major Kovalev's nose had got in the habit of taking a stroll every day, at three o'clock sharp, along Nevsky Prospekt.

As a result, a great many busybodies began flocking to the place and standing there, waiting. If somebody claimed to have seen the nose in, say, Junker's shop, the

crowd would all dash over there, stirring up such a riot that the police had to intervene in force.

One brilliant opportunist who sold stale pastries outside the entrance to the theatre started fashioning solid wooden footstools that he would rent to rubberneckers at eighty kopeks apiece. A staid retired colonel, having renounced his normal afternoon nap, managed to make his way through the crowd with great effort, and what he saw in the window was not the nose but a small painting that had been there for over ten years. It showed a maiden putting on a stocking and a young man spying on her from behind a tree. The colonel left in a huff, shouting that it should be illegal to disturb the public order with stories so stupid.

Another time, rumour spread that the nose was out for a stroll, not on Nevsky Prospekt but in the Tauride Garden. And that it had already been there for a while. A number of students from the Surgical Academy raced to the scene, with the professors leading the way. A distinguished noble lady wrote to the groundskeeper of the Tauride Garden to ask him to show this rare and wondrous phenomenon to the children as well, accompanying her missive with an explanation intended to be instructive and edifying for the young.

Frequenters of high-society salons were quite amused by the affair, making the ladies twitter with their salacious sallies of wit on the subject, which we can easily imagine. A very small number of people were instead displeased for a variety of reasons. A highly cultivated gentleman, for example, wondered disdainfully how, in an epoch so graced by the light of reason, people could still believe in such absurd humbug, and was surprised that the government hadn't immediately looked into the matter. Certainly this gentleman belonged to that category of people who wish the government would get involved in everything, including their daily quarrels with their wives.

But it is time to return to our story. By now you must be convinced that the most incredible and outlandish things can happen in this world. And that sometimes they lack even the slightest hint of realism. So many examples come to mind that it's difficult for me to cite just one. At any rate, by this point you must be aware that I'm very carefully preparing you to learn that all of a sudden, without any rational explanation, in the most indifferent fashion, as if it were nothing, the same nose that had been going around in the uniform of a state councillor and creating such havoc about town, one fine morning, more specifically on 7th April, returned to its proper place, which is to say exactly between the cheeks of Major Kovalev.

But here I must make another ever-so-brief digression.

In the first draft of this story, the final section went as follows: "Besides, everything that has been told was but a dream dreamt by the Major. And when he awoke, he was so cheered up that he jumped out of bed, ran to the mirror and, seeing that everything was in its proper place, started dancing..."

In saying that the story was just a dream, Gogol thus had everything return to the normal and natural order of things. We know, of course, that we sometimes dream the craziest, most unrealistic sorts of things, and so the readers would have been reassured by such an explanation. If it was all just a dream, then nobody would ever be in danger of, say, seeing, from one day to the next, his right foot run off and vanish around a corner.

Then, ingeniously, the author changed his mind.

End of digression. I shall now recount the end that Gogol finally gave to his story.

Nine

On the morning of 7th
April, the Major awoke
and cast a distracted glance
at the mirror. And what
did he see? His nose!
"Well!" he said, putting
his hand on it and holding
it tight, as though fearing
it might disappear again. He
was touching his own nose! He felt
like dancing for joy, but was prevented by
the arrival of his manservant. Collecting
himself, he ordered Ivan to bring him his
things so he could wash, and as he was
washing, he cast another fleeting glance at
the mirror.

The nose was still there.

And as he was rubbing himself with the towel, he kept looking out of the corner of his eye at the mirror.

The nose was still there. He wanted to do a test.

"Have a look yourself, Ivan. I think I have a little pimple on my nose," he said nonchalantly. But meanwhile he was thinking, "What a disaster if Ivan were to say: 'But, sir, not only is there no pimple, there's no nose, either!'"

But in fact Ivan said only:

"There's nothing, no pimple, nothing. Your nose looks good."

At that moment Ivan Yakovlevich the barber appeared in the doorway, though looking as cowed as a cat beaten for stealing something from the pantry.

"I've come to give you a shave, sir," said the barber.

Kovalev remained standing and asked the barber whether his hands were clean.

"Quite clean."

"Liar!"

"By Jove, they're clean, I tell you!"

"Fine, but be careful!" the Major said admonishingly, sitting down.

The barber wrapped him in a towel and, in an instant, with the help of the shaving brush, transformed his face into an enormous whipped-cream pie, of the sort that are brought to the table on a family member's name day. All that was missing were the candied fruits.

"Well, look at that!" Ivan Yakovlevich thought to himself, casting a glance at the Major's nose, then leaning his head to the other side to see it in profile. "Look at that! It looks like his real nose!"

And he kept gazing at it for a while.

Finally, with the utmost delicacy and grace, he raised two fingers with the intention of gripping the nose by the tip, as he was wont to do, to raise his customer's chin.

"Careful!" the Major cried in alarm.

The barber leapt backwards in terror, feeling confused as never before. Then, regaining his courage, he started scraping the Major's neck with his straight razor. And while it felt quite awkward to shave someone under the chin without supporting himself on the person's olfactory organ, all the same, by somehow propping his thumb against the Major's cheek and lower jawbone, he victoriously overcame all obstacles and brought the shave to a conclusion.

When the barber was done, Kovalev got dressed in a hurry, hailed a cab and went straight to a pastry shop. Even before he was at the counter he yelled:

"Hey, garçon, a cup of hot chocolate!"

And at the same time he looked at himself in the mirror.

The nose was still there.

Then he turned around and, squinting a little, cast a haughty glance at one of the two military men present, who had a nose scarcely any bigger than a button on a waistcoat.

Leaving the shop, he went to the secretariat of the ministry to solicit a reply to his request for a post as

vice-governor. In the waiting room, he cast a glance at the mirror.

The nose was still there.

On his way home, he ran into the staff official's wife, Madame Podtochina, who was accompanied by her daughter. His greeting met with an exclamation of joy.

"Therefore," Kovalev said to himself, feeling more and more reassured, "I really have no more defects."

He chatted with the two women for a good while. At one point he even pulled out his snuffbox and voluptuously filled both nostrils with the two of them looking on, all the while thinking to himself, "Would you look at this, ladies, chickens both, look at the fine nose I've got! And, at any rate, good madame, I will not marry your daughter!"

From that day on, Major Kovalev strolled about as though nothing had ever happened, promenading up and down Nevsky Prospekt, going assiduously to the theatre, to ladies' salons and private clubs. His nose, for its part, always behaved in the most upstanding manner possible: it remained on the Major's face, impassive, never giving even the slightest impression that it had ever left that spot. For the rest of his days, the Major was always seen to be in good spirits, cheerful, smiling, elegant, courting without distinction all the lovely ladies he encountered, never missing a single one. Once, he was spotted in a shop that sold uniforms and military decorations, buying a ribbon belonging to a certain order of knighthood, for reasons unknown, since Major Kovalev was not a knight and belonged to no such order.

Epilogue

This is a story that took place in St Petersburg, our northern capital. I could end my tale here, but, having now reached the end, I cannot avoid making a few observations. It would be shirking a specific duty of mine not to do so.

Do you realize how much of this whole business is unrealistic? Do you not agree that both the supernatural detachment of someone's nose from his face, as well as the organ's appearance in various places in the guise of a state councillor, are supremely bizarre? And how could Kovalev not have realized that one cannot place an advertisement concerning the disappearance of a nose in the newspaper? Not because the price of the advertisement would be too exorbitant; that's just silly, and I'm not one to count his pennies. No sir, I'm just saying that it's unseemly and embarrassing. In short, it's not acceptable. Not to mention that such an advertisement could clearly upset the social order.

What's more, how did the nose ever find its way into the just-baked bun? And why wasn't it, too, cooked? And then Ivan Yakovlevich just disappeared without the slightest hint of logic!

But the strangest thing, really, the most inconceivable, is that writers, even good ones, even those admired by the critics, could ever spend their time on such subjects. Of course, everyone is free to imagine whatever he likes, but there are limits, you must admit. Otherwise we truly risk sinking into anarchy! I realize this, it's truly incomprehensible, it's really... No, it's no use. However hard I try, I simply cannot understand it.

Why do people write such things? In the first place, the Fatherland derives no advantage whatsoever from it, nor does the Republic of Letters, as far as that goes. And in the second place... well, in the second place there's no advantage, either.

So: what is to be gained from any of this? What could the consequences be? For what purpose was this story written? What was it trying to prove? No, I really cannot fathom what any of this means.

And yet... It's not that I'm changing my mind, but, all the same... To be honest, yes, I shouldn't want you to think... In short, despite what I have just said, one could, actually, reconsidering the matter... Well, one could admit that sometimes... Yes, there's at least one thing, in the story, that is not, in the end, quite so unbelievable... And if you think about it without preconceptions, there's actually another thing which... And, if you will, even a third... All right, then, in all honesty, let us state it outright: is there anywhere on earth where unrealistic things don't happen? Therefore, if you really think about it, you have to conclude that there is something, after all, deep down, in all of this.

Say what you will, but occurrences of this sort do happen in this world, oh, do they ever!

*This book is dedicated to all grandchildren,
mine and other people's*

WHERE IS THIS
STORY FROM?

Well, it's probably best to see first where its author came from. Nikolai Gogol was born in the Ukrainian Cossack village of Sorochyntsy in the Poltava Governorate of the Russian Empire, on 20th March (in the old calendar), or 1st April (in the new calendar), 1809. (A good excuse, at any rate, for celebrating two birthdays.) His family belonged to the lesser nobility and owned large tracts of land and a village of 400 souls. No reason to be alarmed, though. "Souls" were what one called the poor serfs who were the absolute possession, body and soul, of their owners. Gogol's mother was a woman of strict customs, his father a whimsical *bon vivant*. Nikolai loved his mother deeply, but his father amused him far more.

From an early age, Nikolai proved to have a difficult personality and kept to himself at school, even while winning his schoolmates' sympathies by performing short, amusing monologues that he had written himself. He was a good actor—so good, in fact, that, when he got a little older, for a while he seriously considered becoming a professional actor.

Endowed with a lively imagination, he began writing at a very early age. One day, the well-known poet and playwright Vasily Kapnist, a friend of the family, asked Nikolai to read some of his poems to him. The boy accepted, on the condition that only the two of them should be present, in a closed room. When they came back out, Kapnist said, "A great talent may arise from this little boy." Nikolai was only five at the time, and Kapnist proved correct.

Gogol used his native tongue with great elegance and unequalled refinement, and literary historians still consider him the best stylist in the language. His short stories are utterly perfect. Just think, there isn't a single great Russian writer who hasn't made one of his stories an object of worship. The great poet Pushkin was crazy about "The Nose", Chekhov about "The Carriage", while Dostoyevsky singled out "The Overcoat", stating that all Russian authors, himself included, were born on the tails of that coat.

But Gogol, of course, never admired himself as much as others did. Indeed he was never at peace with himself or the world around him. For a few years he worked as clerk in a ministry, then taught for a while at a university. He was too restless and unhappy to remain for very long in a single place.

He travelled a great deal. He didn't like the society of his day and was ceaselessly portraying, in a pitilessly ironic light, its blind servitude, bureaucratic stupidity and the vain rituals of a fat, ignorant and presumptuous petite bourgeoisie. Around the age of thirty he made his first journey to Italy, finding a bit of serenity in Rome. "I was born here," he wrote to a friend, adding: "I have woken up in my own country."

When he returned to Russia, his mental health declined precipitously. He went through disturbing crises of a mystical-religious nature, to the point where he burned some of his manuscripts... Shortly thereafter, he stopped eating and soon died.

Before him, Russian literature, especially poetry, celebrated great heroes, quasi-mythic figures who lived on earth but seemed to fly high in the sky, as inaccessible as demigods.

Gogol was the very first to write about the little people—the barber, the clerk, the merchant, the humanity one might encounter every day at the market or in an office open to the people—portraying them with pity and irony. With Gogol the world's lower classes burst triumphantly onto the literary stage. Gogol's sarcasm was reserved instead for the petite bourgeoisie and the lower nobility, whom he never spared his judgment.

The manner in which the author deals with these characters is never obtusely realistic; indeed, sometimes his simmering imagination turns reality into a catapult to another reality, that of fantasy. Thus "The Nose" was born.

Personally, as a writer I consider Gogol one of my two literary grandfathers, the other being Lawrence Sterne.

But I'm not the least bit sure they would consider me their grandson.

A.C.

THE CREATORS OF THIS BOOK

ANDREA CAMILLERI (b. Sicily, 1925) is a best-selling and prize-winning Italian theatre and television director and author, perhaps most famous for his Inspector Montalbano series of crime novels. Camilleri has won numerous awards in Italy, France and the UK, and his work has been translated into many languages, including French, German and Japanese.

MAJA CELIJA was born in Slovenia in 1977. She attended primary school during Tito's Yugoslavia, and secondary school during Tuđman's Croatia. She graduated from the European Institute of Design in Milan, and since then her illustrations have travelled all over the world. She now lives in Pesaro, but the forest is her second home: Maja adores the animals and the mushrooms.

SAVE THE STORY is a library of favourite stories from around the world, retold for today's children by some of the best contemporary writers. The stories they retell span cultures (from Ancient Greece to nineteenth-century Russia), time and genres (from comedy and romance to mythology and the realist novel), and they have inspired all manner of artists for many generations.

Save the Story is a mission in book form: saving great stories from oblivion by retelling them for a new, younger generation.

THE HOLDEN SCHOOL (www.scuolaholden.it) was founded in Turin in 1994 with the idea of creating something unique, and is open to students from all over the world. It looks a lot like a huge house with no lack of space, books and coffee. People study something called "storytelling" there—that is, the secret of telling stories in every possible language: literature, film, television, theatre, comics—all of it with the most outlandish results.

This series is dedicated to Achille, Aglaia, Arturo, Clara, Kostas, Olivia, Pietro, Samuele, Sandra, Sebastiano and Sofia.

PUSHKIN CHILDREN'S BOOKS

Just as we all are, children are fascinated by stories. From the earliest age, we love to hear about monsters and heroes, romance and death, disaster and rescue, from every place and time.

In 2013, we created Pushkin Children's Books to share these tales from different languages and cultures with younger readers, and to open the door to the wide, colourful worlds these stories offer.

From picture books and adventure stories to fairy tales and classics, and from fifty-year-old bestsellers to current huge successes abroad, the books on the Pushkin Children's list reflect the very best stories from around the world, for our most discerning readers of all: children.

For more great stories, visit www.pushkinchildrens.com

SAVE THE STORY: THE SERIES

Don Juan by Alessandro Baricco

Cyrano de Bergerac by Stefano Benni

The Nose by Andrea Camilleri

Gulliver by Jonathan Coe

The Betrothed by Umberto Eco

Captain Nemo by Dave Eggers

Gilgamesh by Yiyun Li

King Lear by Melania G. Mazzucco

Antigone by Ali Smith

Crime and Punishment by A. B. Yehoshua